We Oughta Be in Pictures

A Lesson in Being Yourself

by
Sharon Jehlen

Illustrated by
Warner McGee

SCHOLASTIC INC.

New York Toronto London Auckland Sydney
Mexico City New Delhi Hong Kong Buenos Aires

It was a very ordinary Saturday afternoon for the Pirates Who Don't Do Anything. They munched on cheese curls and searched for ones that were shaped like U.S. presidents.

Around 3 o'clock, Pirate Lunt and Larry decided to play a game of tic-tac-toe on Pa Grape's hat. But when Pa Grape woke up, the game ended quickly. It was back to cheese curls—what a bummer!

"I'm tired of doing nothing," Larry said. "Let's *do* something for once."

Pirate Lunt and Pa Grape couldn't believe their ears. "But we're the Pirates Who Don't Do Anything!" they gasped. "We—don't do anything."

"Except admire our impressive collection of presidential cheese curls," added Pirate Lunt. "Look, I found a George Washington!"

"Don't get me wrong. Admiring our presidential Cheese Curl Collection is a great way to spend a Saturday afternoon," Larry said. "But wouldn't it be fun to shake the dust off our boots and get out there and do something different for a change?"

"Well, what do you want to do?" Pirate Lunt asked.

"I'd like to go see a movie!" Larry announced. "It's a pirate movie:

The Dazzling Adventures of Swash, Buckle & Frank!"

Swash, Buckle, and Frank—

Larry was on to something!

"If it's a pirate movie, I'm sure it would be okay for us to use some of our free time . . . ," Pa Grape reasoned. "Let's go!"

Larry brushed his tooth. Pirate Lunt trimmed his mustache. Pa Grape wiped the chalk dust off his hat. "Has anybody seen the lint brush?" he asked. "My hat's a mess."

At the movie theater, the three pirates waited in line to buy their tickets. Then they bought a jumbo bucket of buttery-good popcorn. It was big—but they would share.

NOW SHOWING!

The Dazzling Adventures of SWASH BUCKLE & FRANK

TICKET

TICKET

TICKET

TICKET

Of course, the three pirates sat in the very first row to get the best view of their heroes—Swash, Buckle, and Frank.

As the movie began, the Pirates Who Don't Do Anything just couldn't believe their eyes. Swash, Buckle, and Frank were so dashing, so brave, so . . . PIRATEY!

Swash had a leather eye patch and a colorful pet parrot, and he was a great swordsman. Buckle wore tall boots and fancy clothes and swung from the ropes. Frank had a gold tooth and an old treasure map. After two-and-a-half hours of piratey fun, the movie ended. It had been everything the Pirates Who Don't Do Anything had hoped for—and more!

The three pirates walked down the street toward the Pizza Pagoda.

Each one was quietly dreaming of their new hero.

"I've always wanted a pet parrot," sighed Pirate Lunt.

"I wish I had a pair of boots like that," said Pa Grape.

Larry said, "I would look very dashing with a gold tooth, don't you think?"

Larry, Pa Grape, and Pirate Lunt didn't say much else, except when Pirate Lunt said, "Real pirates wouldn't have to walk 12 blocks to get pizza."

The other two looked at each other and shrugged. He was right.

What else could they say?

"Humpf!"

Once inside the Pizza Pagoda, they were still dreaming of the movie.

Pirate Lunt wanted to be a brave pirate like Swash, fighting off bad guys with his sword. But a sword is heavier than it looks!

Pa Grape wished he were handsome and had nice pirate clothes like Buckle. He dreamed of swinging from the ropes. But ropes are pretty tricky if you don't know what you're doing!

In Larry's daydream, his golden tooth shone brightly, as he used his map to find buried treasure—jewels, silver coins, and gold nuggets. But treasure maps are confusing sometimes. It can be hard to figure out which way is north!

While Pa Grape daydreamed, he looked at Pirate Lunt. "You know," Pa Grape said, "if you were off having sword fights with pirates like Black-eyed Pete, I sure would miss watching **Spaceman Stan** with you every afternoon at 4 o'clock."

"Hey, you're right," Pirate Lunt agreed. "I do like **Spaceman Stan**— and it's really fun because we watch it together!"

"And," Pirate Lunt said to Pa Grape, "where would we play tic-tac-toe if you were all dressed up in fancy piratey clothes?"

Pa Grape looked confused. "What are you talking about?" he asked.

"Never mind," said Pirate Lunt.

Then Pirate Lunt looked at Larry and said, "And if you were out searching for buried treasure, who would share my anchovy and pineapple pizza with me?"

"With extra cheese!" Larry said, as he started to smile.

"Yeah, and another thing," added Pirate Lunt. "You might look good in a gold tooth, but I like you best the way you are now."

If a cucumber could blush, Larry would have.

Pa Grape said, "You know, it's fun to go to the movies together and daydream about being piratey pirates, but I'm glad we're *US*."

"Ditto," agreed Larry. "Hey, look! This pineapple chunk looks like Abraham Lincoln!"

How you made me is amazing and wonderful.

I praise you for that . . .

Psalm 139:14